# Watermelon
## MADNESS

Text: Taghreed Najjar
Illustrations: Maya Fidawi
Translation: Michelle and Tameem Hartman

## CRACKBOOM!

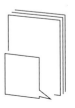

منحة الترجمة
Translation Grant

Noura is a little girl who loves
to eat watermelon.
She eats watermelon
in the morning.

She eats watermelon in the afternoon.

She eats
watermelon
in the evening.

One day, Noura sat down to eat with her family. Mama scooped molokhiya with chicken and rice onto Noura's plate.

But Noura turned up her nose.
"I don't like molokhiya.
I don't like chicken.
I only want watermelon."
"Chicken is good for you, Noura," Baba insisted,
"and molokhiya is yummy!"

Noura roared,
"Watermelon, watermelon!
I only want watermelon!"

Mama was angry and said firmly,
"First eat your molokhiya. Then you
can have watermelon."

That evening, Noura snuck into
the kitchen and saw a big
watermelon sitting on the table.

She stood there for a moment and thought,
"Yum! That is a very big watermelon!
I want to eat it all by myself!"

Noura took the watermelon and rolled it
under her bed so that she could eat it after
everyone had gone to sleep.

She fell asleep thinking about the big watermelon under her bed.

In the middle of the night, Noura felt her bed shaking. She opened her eyes and saw the watermelon growing

bigger and bigger and bigger.

It got so big that her bed almost touched the ceiling.

Noura slid down the watermelon.
"Whee! Whee! I'm so happy,
I'm so happy, this whole
watermelon is all for me!"

Noura walked around the
watermelon and found a door
on its side. She opened the door
and went inside the watermelon.

She walked down a long hallway until she reached
a bright pink room. Inside were
a table and chair made out of watermelon seeds.

Noura sat at the table. "I'm so happy, I'm so happy, this whole watermelon is all for me!"

Noura ate her first piece of watermelon. "Yum, this watermelon is so delicious! I want more." And another piece of watermelon appeared right in front of her.

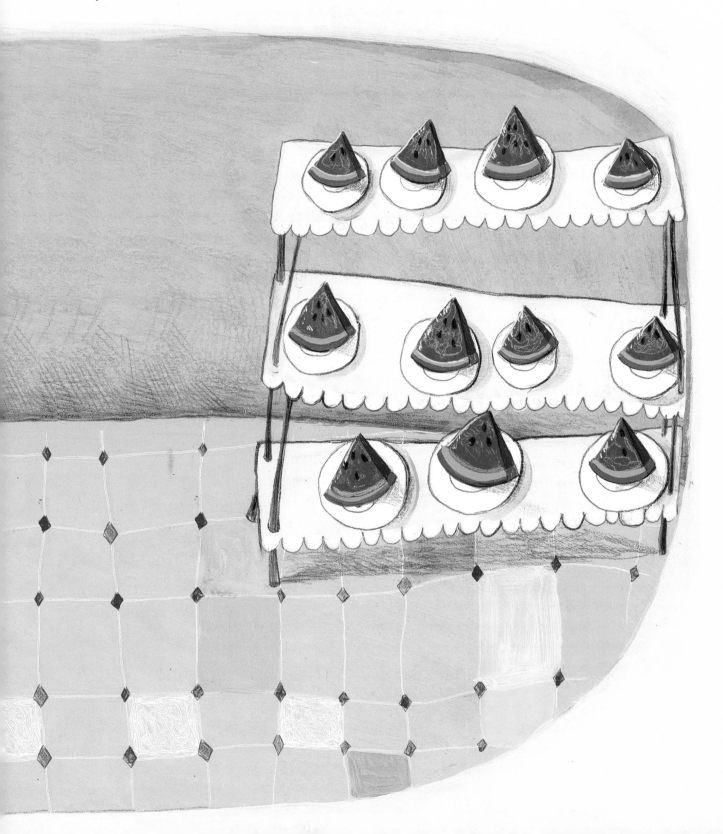

Noura kept eating… and eating… and eating. And she kept saying,
"I want more. I want more. I want more."
The moment she finished a piece of watermelon, another one would appear in its place.

Suddenly Noura stopped eating. She felt herself getting bigger and bigger as the watermelon got smaller and smaller.

Noura grabbed her belly and cried,
"Ow, ow, ow,
my tummy hurts! I don't want any more,
I don't want any more."

Noura opened her eyes and found Mama sitting next to her, and patting her. "What's wrong, Noura? What's the matter?"

"There was a giant
watermelon under
my bed. And I ate
so much of it I felt like
it swallowed me!"

Mama took the watermelon out from under Noura's bed. "Who put this watermelon under your bed, Noura?"

Noura felt embarrassed. "I did.
I'm sorry, Mama. I wanted to eat
the whole watermelon all by myself.
But I started getting bigger and
bigger as the watermelon got
smaller and smaller."

Mama smiled. "Go back to sleep now
Noura, we'll talk about the magic
watermelon tomorrow."
Noura turned over in her bed and fell
asleep right away.

The next morning at breakfast, Noura ate her fried egg and zaatar with olive oil, and drank all her milk.

# Fun facts for watermelon lovers

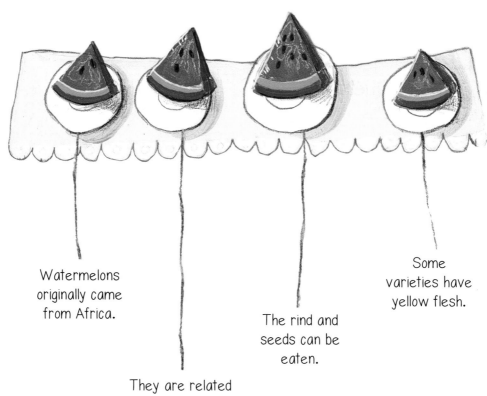

Watermelons originally came from Africa.

They are related to cucumbers.

The rind and seeds can be eaten.

Some varieties have yellow flesh.

# Did you know that?

**Molokhiya**: *molokhiya* refers both to a plant and a traditional Middle-Eastern dish, whose core ingredient is the leaves of the molokhiya, turned into a thick broth or stew and cooked with meat.

**Zaatar**: *zaatar* is a condiment made of dried herbs, spices and seeds including thyme and oregano. It is eaten with bread and olive oil or used as a seasoning for meats and vegetables.

English Edition: © 2018 CHOUETTE PUBLISHING (1987) INC.
Original Arabic Title:Al-baṭṭīhat
Original Arabic Text: © Taghreed Najjar, 2015. All Rights Reserved.
Illustrations: © Maya Fidawi, 2015.
Originally published in the Arabic language by Al Salwa Publishers, Amman, Jordan 2015

CrackBoom! Books is an imprint of Chouette Publishing (1987) Inc.

Text: Taghreed Najjar
Illustrations: Maya Fidawi
Translation: Michelle and Tameem Hartman

Chouette Publishing would like to thank the Government of Canada and SODEC
for their financial support.

**Books**
**Tax Credit**

Gestion
**SODEC**

Bibliothèque et Archives nationales du Québec and Library and Archives Canada
cataloguing in publication

Naǧǧār, Taġrīd Al-
[Baṭṭīhat. English]

Watermelon Madness
(CrackBoom!)
Translation of: Al-baṭṭīhat.

ISBN 978-2-924786-22-2

I. Fidāwī, Māyā. II. Hartman, Michelle. III. Title. IV. Title: Baṭṭīhat. English.
PJ7952.A33B3713 2018          j892.7'37          C2017-941648-0

© 2018 Chouette Publishing (1987) Inc.
1001 Lenoir St., Suite B-238
Montreal, Quebec  H4C 2Z6 Canada
**crackboombooks.com**

Printed in Malaysia
10 9 8 7 6 5 4 3 2 1  CHO2022 DEC2017